CAR WASH WISH

Sita Brahmachari

CAR WASH WISH

Barrington Stoke

For all those who have meandering minds

First published in 2016 in Great Britain by
Barrington Stoke Ltd
18 Walker Street, Edinburgh, EH3 7LP

www.barringtonstoke.co.uk

Text © 2016 Sita Brahmachari
Illustrations © 2016 Louise Wright

A CIP catalogue record for this book is available
from the British Library upon request

ISBN: 978-1-78112-523-6

Printed in China by Leo

CONTENTS

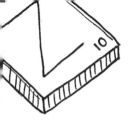

1.

HI THERE, ZED, I'M YOUR BROTHER

If I was a letter, I would be a Z, even though my name starts with an H.

H for Hudson. If we're going to be talking, then you need to know my name.

Today feels more zed-ish than most days.

It's not every day that you –

- Go to your grandad's funeral

- Find out your mum and her boyfriend are going to get married, and sooner rather than later because .... Wait for it ... Here's the final bow on this bundle of news ...

- I'm going to have a half-brother or half-sister – that's you. You'll be here in just under 8 months' time, if – as Mum says – "all goes well".

I already knew that I had to go to the funeral and I had just about got my head around that. But the triple whammy of news just about made my brain explode. That's what I mean when I say it's a zed-ish sort of day.

You might not think about Zs, but I do. When you first look at a Z, it might seem all balanced. Two straight lines linked with a diagonal one. Well, don't be fooled. It's the kind of letter that could topple over or spin faster and faster into a spiral and land as an N. This would not be a good thing because N is a letter I've never liked. N is for "no" and "nerd" and "nutter" – words that make me feel like a "nothing".

I bet you think I'm weird – most people do. Well, since you're going to be my half-brother or half-sister you'll just have to get used to the way I think. Louis says I have a way of seeing things that other people don't, and so I should think about what I *can* do – not what I can't. Louis is your actual dad and, by the time you're born, he'll be my official step-dad.

What I'm not very good at is talking to people and understanding what they mean, because my mind wanders off into zed-ish stuff all the time.

Louis says I should remember that the way my brain works lets me into different worlds. When Louis says stuff like that, I think it makes Mum love him even more. It's Louis's job to work with people who think zed-ish thoughts of one kind or another, so I suppose he *should* understand.

I feel sorry for my real dad because I reckon he's a bit like me ... he can't put thoughts into words like Louis can. Not so they come out right and impress Mum anyway.

The weird thing is, Zed, that it's so easy to talk to you and you don't even exist yet out here in my world. So maybe Louis is right – when I don't have to concentrate I should go with the flow and let my mind wander. I suppose I don't have to deal with you saying anything back, and I don't have to focus on what you might be thinking or what your face and body is telling me because you haven't even really got much of a body or a face ... yet! Can you even think?

I might not be able to read people, but I can read words quite well. I'm faster than most of the people in my class at finishing a book, but sometimes I haven't got a clue what the writer's on about.

So – I bet you're wondering why I call you Zed. Well, Mum calls you a "zygote". I know you're a baby-to-be, but she's being cautious in case anything goes wrong. It makes you sound more like something from outer space, an alien coming to take over ... but maybe that's exactly what you are.

Zygote feels like a zed-ish name. My high-word-score, zed-ish brother or sister. I'll explain about high word scores.

One time, Dad, Mum and me were on holiday in Wales. It rains loads in Wales, so we played a lot of Scrabble. I'm the best at it – I'll teach you one day. I'm a real dictionary nerd. Once I looked up how many words in English have a Z in them. It's 1,413.

That's a lot, I know – but it's true! Check it out when you get born and you learn to read, if you don't believe me.

I know you don't know a single word yet, Zed, but on the scale of things 1,413 is not *that* many words. One day you'll know millions of words. For that reason, Z is one of only two letters in Scrabble that get you a score of 10. (F.Y.I. – the other one is Q.) Z words have a bit of an edge to them – they're not everyday words at all.

Look, I'll go and get my dictionary.

Here it is.

Let's look for some words with Z in them.

In Scrabble, the word doesn't have to begin with Z – all words with a Z in them are high score, and I reckon they deserve to be. When I write them down it helps me to remember them. Things like "AlZheimer's" and "Zygote". Those are words that you might not understand unless you looked them up ... or your grandad had Alzheimer's or your mum had just told you the "great" news about the zygote growing in her belly that might turn into a baby.

When I was learning to write I always found it hard to get my head around the Z.

Head
Bed
Zed

(Do you like that rhyme? Babies like rhymes, so maybe zygotes do too.)

When I put my pen on the paper I have to be very careful not to think of an S, which is just about the worst thing I can do, because it sends me in the wrong direction with the letter. If you think about Z and S they are sort of opposites – if the S wasn't curvy. But then, Zed, you don't know about any of this stuff yet.

So my dictionary says that this is what you are –

Zygote

1. *(Biology) the cell resulting from the union of an ovum and a spermatozoon*

2. *(Biology) the organism that develops from such a cell*

Let's just look at the Z and ignore the gross-out rest of it.

If you do turn into an actual baby that gets born then I could teach you all this stuff about words and letters and what they mean.

But Mum and Louis say, "You mustn't get too excited, it's very early days," and, "It might not happen."

I said to Mum, "Like that time it didn't happen when you and Dad were together."

She pulled a face and didn't answer me, so I suppose I must have said the wrong thing. No matter what they say, Zed, I still can't stop thinking about who you might be one day.

That's why I'm sitting on my bed looking up "zygote" in the dictionary instead of getting ready for Grandad's funeral.

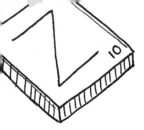

2.

FEELS LIKE THERE SHOULD BE A Z IN ASPERGER'S

"Hurry up, Hudson!" Mum yells from downstairs. "What on earth are you doing up there?"

Talking to a kind of cell called a zygote about the letter Z would be the correct answer. But I don't answer. I write down "AlZheimer's".

That's what my grandad had.

So, Zed, I'll tell you a bit about him because you'll never meet him on account of how he died last week.

Now AlZheimer's is an odd-looking word, you've got to admit. I think it was someone's name. They do that quite often – give medical conditions the same name as the person who discovered them. So you know that someone called Alzheimer discovered the thing that caused Grandad's memory to short-circuit. Just like it was Mr Hans Asperger from Austria that gave his name to what I've got. This is the kind of stuff I know.

But I'd put a Z in Asperger's to make it look more like the way it feels to be me – AZperger's. It's definitely more zingy with a Z.

It's a strange thing living with someone for so long, like we lived with Grandad and still not really know the person at all. I've looked Alzheimer's up lots so that I can understand what it is ...

This explanation doesn't cover the half of it.

Alzheimer's Disease

A common form of dementia believed to be caused by changes in the brain. Begins in late middle age in most cases. Causes memory lapses, confusion, emotional instability, and progressive loss of mental ability.

As you'll never meet him, Zygote, I don't mind telling you ...

It was Grandad's Alzheimer's that –

- Made Dad have to give up work so that he could look after Grandad full-time.

- Made Mum think that Dad cared more about Grandad than he cared about her or me.

- Made Mum have to be out of the house working all hours to "keep this family afloat" (whatever that means).

It was Grandad's Alzheimer's that led Mum to meet Louis too. This was because Dad refused to think there was anything different about me, so Mum took me to the school where Louis works to get assessed. Louis was there and that's how they met.

- After that Dad moved out with Grandad.

- After that the divorce.

- After that Louis moved in.

- And after that ... Zed ... *you* might arrive on the scene now!

So you see what I mean when I say none of these things would have happened if it hadn't been for Grandad's Alzheimer's.

Sometimes I wish that Grandad had died when I was little. Then Mum and Dad might still be together, and then if there was going to be a zygote it could have grown into a real brother or sister, not a half one. Not that I mind that much if you're only half.

Your dad – Louis – he's all right. Even my dad says he's "a good bloke" but we all know they don't "see eye to eye" about me. Dad says him and Louis will have to "agree to differ", and in fact that means they don't agree at all.

Dad doesn't think there's anything different about the way my brain works.

Louis does.

Dad doesn't believe in labels and names for things.

Louis thinks it's useful to know "what we're working with" and he says that when I got assessed it showed I've got Asperger's. He says there's nothing to be ashamed of in having a name for the way my mind works.

But that name – Asperger's – is still one of the main things my mum and my dad argue about even though they're divorced now. Mum's always telling Dad he's "burying his head in the sand". That means not facing up to things that need sorting. Sometimes she yells at him that he's "on the spectrum too" and that makes me feel sad, as if Mum will divorce me one day too.

One time I heard Louis tell Mum off for saying that about Dad and me being on the same spectrum. He said, "That's not helpful to anyone, Pearl."

That was the day I decided that Louis is all right – even though I don't love him like I love my dad or our mum.

Our mum.

That's going to take a bit of getting used to. I've had mum to myself for a long time. Pearl's her name in case you haven't worked that out.

While I've been talking to you, Zed, I've written Zs on every line of this page.

100 Zs x 10 lines = 1000 Zs.

So that's a thousand Zs.

It's a lot of Zs but only 413 less than all the words in English with Z in them. The Zs look quite pretty when they're all joined up, like one of those patterns that make your eyes swim into darting fish shapes even though the pattern isn't really moving at all. That's called an optical illusion. Can you even see yet, Zed?

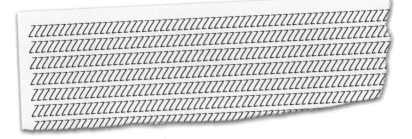

If a conversation could be like the letter Z we'd do a straight line from left to right, then a diagonal, then the bottom line from right to left.

We've done the straight line from left to right –

The bit where we made the connection, where I say, "Hi! I'm Hudson." And you say, "Hi! I'm Zed." (Even though you can't actually talk yet.)

And we've done a bit of diagonal talking, which is talking about stuff we're interested in – well, in this case stuff I'm interested in, but your time will come.

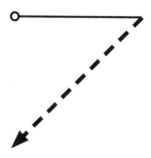

Now we're going back on ourselves and doing the bottom line.

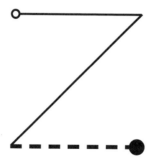

Louis is always teaching me about these ways of putting a structure on conversations to try to make my mind stay focused and stop jumping around everywhere. He calls the way my mind leaps around "kangaroo brain" and he says, "Bring it back, Hudson," when I get lost.

We've finished on the diagonal. So it's time to tell you more about the bottom line.

Now I've had time to think it over, I'm glad Mum and Louis picked today to tell me about you because I've never found this stuff easy to talk to anyone else about. You might even be able to help me cope with today.

You see, funerals are the kind of days when if you're not able to –

Read people's faces

Or

Read people's body language

Then it's even harder than usual to do and say the right thing.

These are the reasons, Zed, why I could really do with someone like you to talk to today.

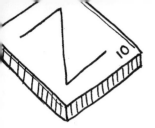

3.

YOUR DAD'S AT THE DOOR

"Hudson, mate, you've got to get dressed. Pearl's a bit stressed out as it is."

Your dad – Louis – is knocking on the door now with a knock that says he's not going away. He opens it and looks in to find me still sitting on my bed in my boxers and T-shirt with my page of Zs. He checks behind him and then steps into my room.

Louis hands me a posh shopping bag – the kind that has cardboard in the bottom so whatever's in it doesn't fall out of shape. I like these kinds of bags. You can flatten and fold them and use them again.

"Here, I bought this for you!" Louis says, and he hands me the bag.

It's a shirt with blue and white stripes, simple but sharp. The kind of shirt that would look good if I had a decent suit to go with it. Now, I know I'm 14 next month (even though everyone thinks I'm about 10) and most kids my age would rather die than wear a suit, but I like the way they make people look all stitched together and sorted. I like neat and I like ironed.

"Thanks for the shirt," I tell Louis.

I fold the bag. It goes nice and flat without me having to make any new folds.

"My pleasure!" Louis says, and he heads for the door.

Did you hear that, Zed? Your dad's all right.

My dad's all right too – it's just I don't see him that much any more. He used to be the person I found it easiest to talk to, but now I don't really have anyone ... except, it turns out, *you*!

Still, it's Grandad's funeral and so, like Mum says, "At least we know for definite he'll turn up today."

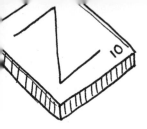

4.

PEOPLE DON'T MEAN WHAT THEY SAY

Socks always on first.

Now for the shirt.

Left arm in.

I wonder if you're left-handed or right-handed, Zed?

Right arm in.

Button up bottom three.

Then top three.

Middle one last.

I check myself out in the mirror.

The new shirt looks good.

I like the thick stripe followed by the thin one. After that there's a middle-sized one. Someone's worked out the pattern just right.

I like looking at clothes online. I've seen a suit that would look perfect with this shirt. It's navy blue, fitted, with drainpipe legs. As soon as we knew Grandad was dying, I found the link again on my laptop. That's that thing on my bed, Zed –

Bed
Zed
Head
Zed!

When you get a bit bigger Mum and Louis say I can come and look at a scan of you on one of those screens in hospital. You won't be wearing anything, but I don't suppose you'll mind.

The suit I picked out for Grandad's funeral looks like the ones rock stars wear sometimes. It's not a boring work suit. It's got style. But when I asked Mum if I could have it, this is what she said.

Bed
Zed
Head
Zed
Mum
Said
Zed

Enough rhymes, sorry. This is what Mum said –

"We'll buy you a suit for our wedding. I don't want to get it too early in case you put on a growth spurt. If you want a suit for the funeral you'll have to ask your dad."

"You don't want me to grow?" I asked Mum.

"No, Hudson," she said. "I just don't want to buy you a suit and then a few months later have to buy another one because you've grown out of it."

"So, you're getting married in a few months then?" I asked. "I won't grow that much in a few months."

"No, Hudson! I didn't say that."

Actually, Zed, she did. This is what's different about me. Most people ... that probably includes you ... most kids learn quite fast that when people say things, they don't always *mean* what they say.

In fact, the way I see it, people hardly ever say exactly what they mean.

Louis says that I need to learn to read a situation. "You have to look at how people act at the same time as listening to what they're saying," he says. "It's a bit of a balancing act."

Then you have to piece it together and work out what the sum of the two – **ACTIONS + SPEECH** – really means.

For some people it's not that hard once they learn to read the codes. For me it's like when I went to this circus skills workshop and this man got up on a rope and started walking along and juggling at the same time. That's how hard it is for me.

But I bet you'll be able to do that, Zed – the de-code thing, I mean. Most people can.

Anyway, I don't know why Mum said that Dad would have to buy the suit because there's no way Dad would be able to afford a suit, and Mum knows that, so she might as well have just said "No!" and have done with it.

Instead of what she actually told me when I asked her straight up.

I said, "Why can't I wear the same new suit for your wedding *and* the funeral?"

"No!" she snapped at me. "Keep the two separate. I'll buy you something new for the wedding. We can adapt your school uniform or something for the funeral."

"ADAPT MY SCHOOL UNIFORM?" I yelled. "Why do you want to keep the two separate?"

But Mum wouldn't answer me.

So that's the story of how I come to be standing in front of my bedroom mirror looking like a plonker in a cool shirt and my school uniform trousers. I pick up my blazer and sling it over my shoulder.

If it was summer I could probably get away with not wearing a blazer at all ... or it would be OK if I had a smart coat. Maybe I could just pretend it's summer instead of ice-cold November.

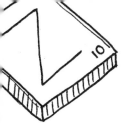

5.

SCHOOL CREST

"I'm not wearing this blazer," I tell Mum as I walk down the stairs. "It looks sad."

"No!" Mum said. "What's sad is that you're worrying about a little thing like your uniform and in the meantime we're going to be late to help your dad set up the wake."

"What's a wake?" I ask.

Mum doesn't answer.

See what I mean, Zed? None of this makes sense. Sorry. This is not a very good way for you to find out about our mum. She's actually really calm most of the time and she almost never shouts like this. I think it's because of you, Zed, that she's got so ratty. I suppose I would get ratty too if I had a zygote growing inside me that kept making me want to throw up.

"Do you need to be sick?" I ask Mum.

"No!" she snaps. "I do not need to be sick, Hudson. Now come on, look lively, and put your blazer on."

"But everyone will think I'm going to school," I tell her. "That's why you told me I had to wear my uniform for school in the first place, so everyone knows I'm going there … But today I'm not going there, so if I wear my blazer people will get confused."

"We haven't got time for this, Hudson!" Mum shouts and she snatches my blazer off me. "If I pick off the school crest it'll look like any other suit."

She grabs some nail scissors and starts to snip around the edges of the crest.

Louis walks in.

"You look smart," he says to Mum, and he brushes a bit of fluff off her jacket.

"Nice shirt!" he says to me. I think that might be a joke because he bought it for me so he would think it looks nice, wouldn't he? I don't know, I don't really get jokes. Jokes are like walking on a tightrope while juggling *and* doing a cartwheel all at the same time.

"The shirt is nice," I agree. "Do you think it needs ironing?"

"No it does not!" Mum snips the last bit of thread from the school crest and lays it on the table.

"There," she says. "It looks ... just like any other blazer jacket now."

"It doesn't," I say as she hands it to me. That's another thing I can't do, Zed – I can't not tell the truth. Lots of people think things but they don't say what they're thinking, but with me ... it just blurts out.

In fact, what my blazer now looks like is a black school uniform jacket with the crest picked off. It's darker in the place that the crest was and all around the edges of the shield shape are holes where the needle has pierced the material of the pocket.

Louis winks at me.

"Why are you winking at me?" I ask him.

"Just go with it, mate," he says, and he winks at me again. "Know what this means?" he asks as he reads out the Latin words on the badge.

"*Lumen accipe et imperti.*"

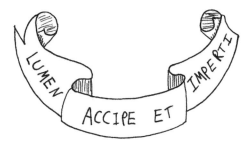

In fact, that was the first thing I looked up when I went to my new school. You might have guessed by now, Zed, that I like looking things up. That's why I know loads more about everything than most people do. Louis says "my curious mind" makes me "clever", but at school it just makes me feel like what they call me – a "nerd".

"It means take the light and pass it on," I tell him.

Louis smiles at Mum when I say this and puts his hand on her stomach.

"Why are you touching Mum's belly?" I ask him.

Mum blushes and squirms away.

"Your school's Latin saying about 'light'. It made me think about the baby," Louis explains.

"We're not calling it a baby yet," Mum whispers to Louis.

"It's a zygote," I tell Louis. "I've called him Zed."

Louis laughs. "So it's a boy and his name's Zed ... is that right, Hudson?"

"Yep!"

Mum and Louis are both laughing now. Sometimes I make people angry and I don't know why. Sometimes I make people laugh and I don't know why either. Sometimes the laughing feels bad, like at school when I don't read things right. I don't mean books – I told you I'm good at reading books, well the words anyway, but I'm no good at understanding the looks people give each other. Sometimes after they've done those looks they laugh and I can hear something in their laughter that makes me feel bad. But this laughing that Louis and Mum are doing now makes me feel good, but I still try to squirm away as they put their arms around me and try to cuddle me.

Even I can see how happy they are that you're coming, Zed.

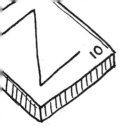

6.

ELEPHANTS IN THE ROOM

Louis is the best at explaining stuff to me about things that I can't see but that might be in the room ... stuff like elephants.

You might not find this kind of thing hard when you grow up, Zed, but I do.

I'm pretty sure you're going to grow up into a boy. That's just how I see you. I'm not sure I would be able to talk to you like this if you were a girl. It would be like it is when I try to talk to Flora. She's the nicest girl I know ... and the fact I like her sort of makes it harder to talk. Anyway, I reckon you'll turn out to be a boy.

So I'll try to explain this thing that your dad told me about how sometimes elephants aren't just in zoos or in India or Africa.

Louis says, "It's a saying – the elephant in the room."

This is how I understand what he tells me. Sometimes there are elephants in rooms, but they're not proper elephants, they're people's feelings. I'm not doing very well with this, am I? When Louis explained ... it was better. I'll start again.

Do you know the saying, "There's an elephant in the room?"

Well, there's not just one elephant in Dad's front room. It feels to me like there's a whole herd of elephants. Even though, if you opened the door into my dad's flat, you would only see –

- a few bare walls

- a few odd bits of furniture

- me, my mum and dad

- a few plates of sandwiches, crisps and cake.

That's all that you would *see*, but I can tell you there's a whole herd of elephants in here, and they walk around in the room and trample everything under their big feet.

But of course no one says anything about the herd of elephants. Instead, we all pretend not to notice.

The elephants are all the things and all the feelings that we're not going to talk about today.

The elephants are also all the arguments Mum and Dad usually have, but have decided not to have today. They are about –

- How angry Mum is that Dad's always missing out on having me over.

- How much Mum thinks Dad gave up on us because Grandad was ill with his Alzheimer's.

But I'm glad that there are only elephants in the room because the elephants are quieter than the arguments.

So, Zed, that's what you do with elephants in rooms – you ignore them because you can't deal with them all. And when you have a great big herd of elephants in your front room you realise just how huge they are.

So the reason why I'm here in my dad's flat with my mum and dad together – which almost never happens now – is because we're getting ready for Grandad's wake.

It was only on the way over here that Mum got round to telling me what a wake is.

It's a weird word – a "wake".

It's not "awake" as in when you're not asleep, which is, come to think of it, Zed, what I bet *you* do most of the time – sleep.

But *a wake*.

It's sort of like a tea party after the funeral.

So here I am, sitting in my dad's flat at the table where only a few days ago my grandad would have been sitting too. I'm watching my mum and dad walk around the room organising stuff like –

- Napkins
- Paper plates
- Cups and saucers
- Extra chairs
- Plates of cakes
- Plates of sandwiches
- Crisps
- Biscuits.

If I didn't know that it was a wake, and Mum and Dad weren't being so miserable with each other, then I could almost imagine that this was a birthday party.

But a wake is the exact opposite of a birthday party.

As Mum explained, a wake is just when you invite people back for tea after a funeral. It seems a bit grim to me ... a "funeral day party". Even though the word "fun" is contained in the word "funeral" it really doesn't feel like it, because today is just about the most miserable that I have ever seen Mum and Dad be with each other.

I told you already, Zed, that Grandad was always the main reason why Mum and Dad argued. Well, he's not here any more but you can sort of see them arranging all the things they ever thought and said about him in their minds as they lay out the plates of cakes.

This room is full of all the elephant-arguments they ever had about him.

"I was fond of him, you know?" Mum says, and she looks over to the chair where Grandad used to sit.

Dad nods and swallows so his Adam's apple – that's the sticky-out lump in your throat you have when you're a boy – moves down and up again.

It was nearly always Mum who had the arguments about Grandad. She used to get angry about Grandad and say all that stuff she used to say –

"You can't let him take over our lives like this."

"We can't cope."

"It's not fair on Hudson."

"It's not fair on me!"

"It's not even fair on Harry!" (That was my Grandad's name) "He needs proper care."

"You'll lose your job."

"I need to get out of here."

"I need to work."

"I can't stand his outbursts."

"I can't have him live here any more."

"It's not good for Hudson."

"He'll have to go into a care home."

"Look what he's broken this time!"

"There's going to be nothing left to break soon. We can't carry on like this ..."

Mum walks over, takes my hands away from my ears and smiles at me. Sometimes I think she can hear the noise that gets into my head too.

"It's very bare in here," Mum says to Dad. "Don't you want to put some pictures up?"

Dad looks up at the walls. "I suppose I could do," he says, as if he's never thought about it before.

"If Hudson's going to come and stay more often you'll have to brighten the place up a bit," Mum tells him.

Dad looks over at me.

"There'll be a spare room now, won't there?" Mum asks.

Dad nods.

Mum's phone rings.

"Hi darling!"

When she says "darling" it's always Louis. Mum never calls Dad "darling". Not now, not ever. I can't remember a time when she called him that.

Mum walks into the other room so she can talk to Louis "in private".

For a few minutes, me and Dad sit at the table and look at the cakes and listen to Mum talking to Louis. I get this picture in my head of all the elephants in the room heading for the table and scoffing all the food in one go.

"Yes, I'm sure Austin won't mind," Mum says. "Come back for the wake afterwards. I'm going to need you."

While I think about elephants, Dad stares at a photo of Grandad when he was young. He looks a bit like Dad does now. He's standing in a car factory that looks like a big metal barn, with a woman who I've been told is my grandma. I never met her because she died before I was born. Dad said that the factory is the place where Grandad and Grandma met.

I wish I could think of something to say to Dad.

"Why do they call it a wake, Dad?" I ask. "Why isn't it just a funeral tea?"

Dad looks up at me. "I don't know, son. I think in the old days they used to keep the coffin in the house and people used to watch over it, before it was buried."

"That's gross. Why would they do that?"

"Why don't you ask Louis? I bet he'll know."

It's true. I bet Louis will know. I'll ask him later.

I can't think of what else to say, so Dad and me just sit and listen to Mum talking to Louis.

Dad picks up a sandwich and chews it as we listen.

It's tuna. Dad doesn't like tuna. He pulls a face like he wants to spit it out.

"I know you do, darling," Mum says. "I love you too. I'll see you later. Will do. Love you, Lou, love you … you too."

Dad swallows his last mouthful of tuna sandwich and pushes his plate away. He looks like he's going to be sick.

Sometimes I think I could make things better.

I get this idea now that it would be best if I tell Dad about you, Zed. I think the news about you will sound better coming from me.

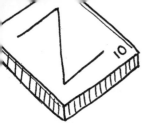

7.

FUNERAL CAR

After the struggle with the tuna sandwich and the phone call with Louis, there's a knock on Dad's door.

When Dad opens it, a man in a long black coat is standing there. He looks like a crow. He keeps his head bowed the way Louis told me you should never do if you're talking to people. But the crow-man doesn't say anything. We just follow him outside.

There is a long black car with flowers on top that Dad says is called a "hearse". The flowers aren't just any old flowers. Dad's had them made in the shape of a car – and it looks brilliant. It's this old-fashioned sports car with crazy headlights like frog eyes. They've made the headlights with yellow flowers. The rest of the car is made out of cream flowers. Dad walks up to get a closer look and Mum follows.

On the back of the flower car there is a sort of registration plate with "Austin Healey 1" written in red rose buds.

"That's brilliant," Mum says, and she squeezes Dad's arm. "Harry would have loved that."

The Grandad that Mum is talking about, who would have loved this car, if he was still alive, is the Grandad I never knew. But Mum and Dad did.

When I think about it, I realise that this is one of the few things I know for sure about Grandad – how much he used to love cars.

Sometimes Dad used to try to rally Grandad out of his silences by talking about stuff and showing him photos from when Dad was a little boy, growing up. Sometimes, if Dad watched a car programme with him, Grandad would start to talk about some engine he remembered fixing.

But in the end Dad had to stop doing this because Grandad went crazy with him, and ranted and raved at him about how disgusting it was that Dad had let his car get so filthy dirty. And I don't know what that had to do with anything.

The crow-man is the driver of the funeral car and he's talking to my dad. His head isn't bowed any more and they are both looking at the flowers.

"My wife ... she's the florist," he explains. "She says she's never had to do anything this ornate before. Took her hours and hours it did." The driver smiles. "I hope you like it, lad."

"What's ornate?" I ask, but no one tells me. I'll look it up later.

It sounds funny, the way the crow-man calls my dad a "lad". It means that there are more rhyme words that I can put together for you, Zed ... These are the sorts of words you'll learn to read first.

Zed
Head
Zed
Mum

Said
Zed
Dad
Lad

We walk to the car behind the funeral car, the one that's called a "hearse".

Dad is biting his bottom lip and looking at his shoes. He doesn't want to show anyone that he's got tears in his eyes.

"The flowers are beautiful," Mum says, and she touches Dad's hand.

"Do you still love each other?" I ask, but as soon as it's out I know I shouldn't have asked that.

They both pretend they haven't heard me.

"You've cleaned the car then!" Mum says, as Dad holds open the passenger door for her.

She shakes her head to say "no" and opens the back door for herself. "You two boys ride up front together," she says. "I'll take the back seat."

I switch on the radio and the music comes out too loud. Dad bashes the knob and the music's gone.

Dad is staring at Grandad's coffin in the hearse ahead of us, and Mum is staring at her black shiny gloves. I think the elephants must have climbed into the car with us when we weren't looking, and now we are all crushed in together with the things that no one can find the words to say.

See, Zed. I'm not the only one who finds this communication thing difficult.

It's not that far to the church where Grandad's going to be buried. I've been there before, but somehow the road seems to have stretched itself into an enormous runway of tarmac. It just goes on and on and on with only one car in front of us (if you don't include the flower car), and a long line of them behind us.

"Can't crow-man speed up a bit?" I ask.

"Shhh!" Mum says. "Don't call him that! We're going slow to show our respect."

Slow means respectful? I don't see why.

Then Mum looks in the side mirror, turns around, checks out the car behind and waves.

"There's your brother," she tells Dad.

Maybe Dad doesn't hear her because he doesn't react.

"What happens to all the flowers after the funeral?" I ask Dad into the silence.

"We leave them on the grave," Dad answers.

"Even the flower car?" I ask.

"Especially the flower car," Dad says.

"But Grandad won't see them," I say.

Mum taps me on the arm quite hard. That means "Enough, Hudson!" and that I should be quiet.

I don't say anything else, Zed, but I wonder if Dad really understands that Grandad is dead. How's a dead person going to care one way or another about the flowers? Even if they are flowers made into the shape of an Austin Healey, which was Grandad's favourite car. A dead person can't see the flowers, can they?

Then, if I really think about it, I realise I can't see you either, Zed, but I care about you already.

"I get it!" I say to Dad. "It's so everyone knows how much you loved Grandad, isn't it?"

Dad nods and bites his lip hard again, but the tears fall out of his eyes anyway.

I add another word to the rhyme.

Dad
Lad
Sad.

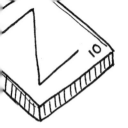

8.

CAN'T BE HERE TO SEE THIS

There are a lot of long shiny black cars at Grandad's funeral. I must be getting more into Dad's way of thinking now, because an idea pops into my head.

"Shame Grandad can't be here to see this," I say.

I get this memory flash of Dad trying to get Grandad to think about stuff from his past.

In the memory, we're back in our front room and it's the way it used to look before Louis decorated.

The TV's on. We're watching a car programme together and Grandad perks up when the presenter talks about Coventry and somewhere in America called Detroit where there used to be lots of car factories too.

"D'you know, son," Grandad says in my memory. "Coventry was the Detroit of the British car industry?" It sounds a bit like he's saying words from an advert.

"Remember how you took me around the factory?" my dad says to Grandad.

Grandad says nothing – not so much as a flicker.

I almost forgot where I am right now. I tell Dad, "I don't know that much about Grandad, really."

Dad looks at me. "I should have told you more about him," he says. "When you come over I'll tell you some stories of when I was growing up and show you some photos."

"Why didn't you show me before he was dead?" I ask.

Dad doesn't answer.

And so I try to add up the actual things that I know about Grandad –

- He worked in a car factory all his life.

- He met my grandma there.

- He loved cars. Louis doesn't have a car. He's all into being eco and he calls people who love cars "petrol heads". So I suppose Grandad was a petrol head.

- He got Alzheimer's.

- He must have *really* loved cars, because he named his son (my dad) Austin, after the Austin factory he used to work in.

Dad always used to joke that he was lucky he wasn't called Mini or Rover or Rolls.

As I told you, Zed, I don't get jokes that easily. But I used to like the feeling when Dad told them, because I could see that they made him feel happy. I haven't heard him tell a joke for a very long time, not even one of what Mum calls his "car crash Christmas cracker" ones. But I suppose that's because we're never together at Christmas any more.

I hope Dad kept telling Grandad jokes after they moved out together.

I feel Dad's arm around me.

"You look smart," he tells me.

"I don't. I look weird," I say.

"Me too!" Dad sort of laughs.

It's true. He doesn't wear clothes like this normally.

His clothes are –

- A long woolly coat

- A brown silky scarf

- Smart black trousers (a bit too shiny)

- Very shiny black shoes (a bit too tight for him I would say, by the way he's walking)

- Aftershave that gets up my nose and makes him smell nothing like himself.

I like Dad better in his greasy overalls.

"Don't be too sad," Dad says. "Grandad didn't have much of a life in the end."

I shrug away from him.

Now that Dad doesn't live with us any more what I miss from our house is his smell – oil and soap. I always used to smell that when he came in. Mum did too and she didn't like it – she used to order him straight upstairs to scrub up. But sometimes, when I was little, I used to stand in the hall and breathe in the engine grease that meant that Dad was home.

Today, even his nails are shiny for the funeral, with no sign of dirt or oil under them.

Today Dad looks clean and ... heavy ... like a big grey rock. And his face is wet with tears.

I suppose Grandad was Dad's dad and most people would cry at their dad's funeral ... even if what I heard Mum say to Louis is true.

Mum said that now Dad doesn't have to look after Grandad any more he can open his old garage again and "get a life".

That reminds me. There's one other thing about Grandad that I do know. It's quite a big thing actually – elephant-sized, I'd say.

I've given you your name, Zed, and my grandad gave me mine.

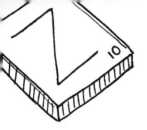

9.

HOW I GOT MY NAME

This is how the story goes.

Mum was pregnant with me, just like she's pregnant with you, Zed. Only she had a big belly bump, not just the sort of belly that makes people say, "Has she put on a bit of weight?"

Anyway, Mum was having a sit-down on the sofa.

Grandad was watching a thing on TV about the Hudson River and he comes out with this –

"Do you know, Pearl, I always had this dream when I was a boy of going to New York, standing on the George Washington Bridge, and tossing a coin into the Hudson River?"

Mum says she wasn't really listening because that's how Grandad's Alzheimer's started – he burbled on about nothing very much.

But then he placed his hand on her bump like Louis did to Mum this morning (even though she hasn't got much of a bump yet).

And after that, Grandad pulled a penny from his pocket and threw it up in the air so it landed on the other side of the room.

"I reckon that's the nearest I'll ever get to that river," he said. "But Hudson's a great name. Don't you think so, Pearl?"

So it's Grandad who I have to thank for my name. I like it that my name is an actual river. Not just any old river either, but one that flows all the way through New York City. Even if Grandad never got to stand on that bridge – one day I want to.

So ... this is the sum of the actual facts that I know about my grandad.

But what did Grandad know about me?

'Nothing much,' I think, 'and by the end he even forgot my name.'

Dad is helping to carry Grandad's coffin inside now and we are all following on behind. Four men are carrying Grandad on their shoulders. I know that one of them's my uncle, my dad's brother, but I've never seen the other two before. Perhaps they are old friends. I wish Dad had asked me to help him carry Grandad. I know I don't know that much about him, but I know more than them and I'm stronger than I look.

There is organ music playing that never really tunes to the note it's reaching for.

In my mind I see this big wide river.

I'm standing in the middle of the bridge with Grandad, looking down. My head swirls and I am all dizzy.

I place a hand in my pocket.

Grandad places his hand in his pocket.

We count –

"1, 2, 3 ..."

We let go together.

"Make a wish!" Grandad says, and then we throw our shiny copper coins and watch them fly through the air in a great glittery arc.

Sun dances on the water.

Then the coins disappear into the Hudson.

"Hudson," Dad whispers. "Shift over."

I'm sitting in the church. Mum, Dad and me are close together. Mum edges past Dad to my other side so she doesn't have to sit next to him.

I look down at Dad's lap. "Why are your hands shaking?" I ask.

I think my voice might be too loud because Mum gives me an evil stare and puts her finger to her lips – even I know what that means. "Quieten down, Hudson. Shut up!"

The vicar says a few things about kingdoms and Heaven. We get up to sing a song I've never heard of and sit down to take a moment of "silent thought" about Grandad. It's weird, Zed, but when someone tells you to think about someone you can't think of anything. I can't even picture Grandad's face. After all that silent thought, Dad gets up and walks to the front of the church with his shaky hands to make his speech. He looks at Mum, but she still seems to be really interested in her gloves.

I haven't heard that many people making speeches but even I can tell that Dad's speech about Grandad is only about a "2" on a scale of 1–10. And I've only given him those 2 points because he's my dad and I love him.

What he says is more gaps than speech, but then when I think of Grandad that seems about right because Grandad's mind was full of gaps too.

This is more or less what Dad says.

"He was my dad."

"I loved him."

"We ..."

He looks at Mum and me – so I think we are supposed to be the "we" even though we're not really "we" any more.

"We ... tried to look after him as best we could after Mum died."

"He loved Mum. He was devoted to her. Never really got over her dying ... and he loved cars of course and me and my brother Healey ... In no particular order!"

Dad smiles and a little laugh goes around the church at the sound of his brother's name ...

"He loved cars enough to call us after his favourite ones!"

Dad nods towards my uncle and my cousin, who I don't really know, and then he points to the flower car on top of the coffin. Then he carries on.

"My dad taught me all I know about being a mechanic and he encouraged me to open my own garage … There were a few precious moments to remember that were just his and mine …"

Then, when you think he's getting into the swing of this speech thing, Dad starts crying and coughing and almost runs back to our pew. Mum hands him a tissue really fast like she wants him to stop. I don't see why. If my dad died I would cry, too.

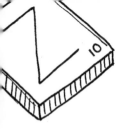

10.

MAKING OUR OWN WAY

Outside the church the vicar chats to everyone as if she knows them, but she doesn't.

I hear people say, "It was a lovely service," even though it wasn't.

See what I mean, Zed – people don't always say what they think.

The vicar shakes hands with my dad and pats him on the back. I hear her say something like, "Not to worry. Words are never enough, not for any of us."

Mum nods. "That's right, never enough," she says.

I can't tell if she's still being kind to Dad or not.

All around there are ladies in navy blue and black hats sorting out who will get a lift back to Dad's flat with who, and in which shiny car.

I notice lots of people are chatting to Uncle Healey and Ford (that's the name of my cousin who I don't really know), and they keep looking over at me. Ford looks like the lead singer out of that boy-band the girls at school like. Well, most of them … Flora says she thinks he's "all hype". She says she can see right through those sorts of people.

"Is your brother older or younger than you?" I ask Dad.

"Older."

"He looks younger," I tell Dad.

"Thanks!"

Dad laughs, but I don't think he's really happy for me to think that.

Ford is walking over to us now. He's wearing a proper suit. The kind I wanted. He's not looking at me – he's looking down at my pocket where the crest used to be. I put my hand up to cover the holes where the stitches were.

"Hey! I'm cousin Ford! So sorry about your grandad," Ford says and he holds out his hand for me to shake.

"We know who you are," I say.

I don't take his hand because I don't think shaking hands is something you do with your cousin. He might be taller than me, but in fact he is younger.

Anyway, I'm still covering up the pocket of my blazer with my hand-shaking hand.

Ford gives up on the handshake thing and lets his arms drop by his sides.

"Why did you say you're sorry about *my* grandad?" I ask. "He was your grandad too."

Dad elbows me as if I've said something I shouldn't have. But I'm just stating the facts, Zed. You'll learn. Sometimes you're not allowed to state the facts, because apparently the facts can seem rude.

"Sure!" Ford says. "Anyways, Dad's asking if you guys want a lift."

Ford points over to the swanky hire car that Dad told me was waiting for them at the airport when they landed.

"No thanks. We've made our own way this far," Dad says.

Ford looks at Dad and nods at him. He's doing that sort of nodding that makes it clear that everyone else understands what's being said except me.

"Well, see you in a while!" Ford says to me and walks over to his dad, who is chatting to the ladies in the hats and making them smile.

Dad stares at Healey. "I expect he's got lots of catching up to do," he mutters to himself, and he stares hard at them like he's forgotten I'm here.

"Should I come with you then, Dad?" I ask.

"OK," Dad says. "But I'm not taking anyone else."

Uncle Healey looks over to Dad and me and waves.

I wave back, but Dad keeps his hands in his pockets.

I take Dad's arm and lead him to his car. On the way, I catch Mum's eye. She smiles at me like she thinks I'm doing the right thing, staying with Dad.

Louis says he thinks sometimes I have flashes of brilliance and I'm getting a bit better at understanding stuff that other kids wouldn't even begin to understand. I don't know about that, but I think I might be getting a bit better than Dad at working out what's best to do.

When we get in the car Dad starts up the engine straight away, but the glass is all fogged up inside so we're not going anywhere until the ice-mist clears from the screen.

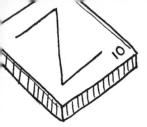

11.

CLEARING THE SCREEN

When Mum and Dad were together I didn't used to go around thinking much about time. Now I do, because the time I spend with Mum and with Dad is supposed to get shared out. At least, that's what Mum tries to do.

Sometimes I think Mum likes it when Dad calls to cancel at the last minute and lets her down *again*. She always says it's me that he's letting down, but he's letting her down too. And that's one of the ways she can be sure that she did the right thing when she split up from him.

But you don't need to worry, Zed. Louis is never late. He never cancels. He's 100% reliable. But no matter how nice and kind and how reliable and steady he is ...

He's still not my dad.

So, I'm in the car with Dad and the ice-mist is taking its time to clear from the screen. "Dad!" I say. "Can we go on holiday to New York, just you and me?"

Dad looks a bit surprised by the question. Then he starts to cry again. You know what, Zed? I wish the thought about New York had never jumped into my head because I feel so bad inside to see my dad this upset.

Zed
Head
Zed
Bed
Wed
Mum
Said
Zed
Dad
Lad
Bad
Mad
Sad
Sad
Sad

I don't feel like rhyming any more.

My frozen-twig toes are warming up from the heater under the dashboard. It makes a burny, tingly feeling.

"Let everyone else go first," Dad says, as if he's talking to himself.

A little space clears on the windscreen in front of us in the shape of a comma.

A baby Zed.
With an oversized head.
Its spine all curly and
Its legs tucked under.

"Mum's having a Zygote!"

I don't even know I've said this out loud until Dad turns to me. His mouth has fallen open so I can see the pink gum space of his missing molar tooth. His face is all lined. He looks old.

"A *what?*" he asks.

"A baby," I tell him.

He closes his mouth just as I'm thinking, 'I wish I could keep my mouth shut.'

And then a deep moan comes from Dad's throat. It sounds just like next door's bull dog that sets up a long low whine when it gets lonely.

"A baby? Is that so?" is all Dad says.

He breathes in deep, releases the hand brake and we drive away.

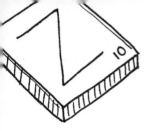

12.

THE WRONG ROAD

"Where are we going?" I ask Dad as we turn right. He doesn't answer.

But I'd noticed that all the other cars took a left turn out of the church. We seem to be driving away from Dad's flat where Grandad's funeral tea party is waiting.

We drive till the houses turn to fields. Not total countryside, but those kinds of fields that are in between the country-type fields and the town-type fields. I think I read somewhere that lots of these fields together are called a green belt. The picture that comes into my head when I think about this is of a fat city being pulled in tight by a big green belt.

At last, Dad slows the car and pulls into a run-down forecourt. It has a hand-painted sign that says "Moore's Garage" outside.

"I used to drive out here with your grandad," Dad says, and he jumps out of the car. "Won't be long!"

I see him chatting to an old man who's holding onto Dad's hand and shaking his head.

"Dad, what are we doing here?" I ask when he opens the door again, but Dad just starts up the car and drives around to the car wash.

"Want to know where I went in my head when I should have been giving the speech I'd planned about Grandad's life?" Dad asks.

I nod.

"I came right here to Moore's Garage car wash."

On the sign for the car wash it says it takes 5 minutes for a deluxe wash. Dad says it actually takes 5 minutes 42 seconds. The 42 seconds are for the bit after the brushes stop whirring.

"That's when the car wash lowers the car and the light turns from red, to amber, to green. Then you're free to drive away. That's the bit that takes 42 seconds."

"How do you know that ... about the seconds?" I ask, but I don't think he hears me.

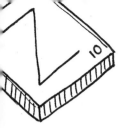

13.

SHELLS

We have to wait our place in the car wash queue and Dad's curled back inside his shell.

From where I'm sitting I can see the yellow and red Shell sign and I wonder who came up with that as a logo for a business that sells petrol and oil. I will have to look that up later. Symbols and metaphors and stuff like that are things I find really hard to understand, Zed. But my mind gets a bit fixed on them, so sometimes I can't think of anything else until I've got a hold of why they're there and what they mean.

I think that perhaps what the Shell sign people were trying to do was to make petrol seem natural, part of the earth, not something that turns into poison and pollution. I bet that's how they do it – by linking thoughts. Shells come from the sea and oil comes from under the sea ...

so instead of thinking of birds with their feathers all clogged with oil, the shell makes people think of something natural and pure and washed clean by the sea.

Clever how they can move what things mean by putting ideas together that would never normally go together. I think I could be quite good at that. Maybe it's what I'll do one day.

These are the sorts of links that the short circuits in Grandad's mind stopped him making. I think how scary it must be when you can't make anything add up, or when you can't link words to things at all ... not even your own memories.

I remember how, before Grandad's Alzheimer's got really bad, he sort of knew he was forgetting things. He said it felt like everything he thought of as "him" was floating away. One time, he told me about this dream he had that really scared him. In the dream, Grandad was sitting on a chair but all people could see was his coat.

I laughed when he said that, but it wasn't as stupid as it sounded. Now I think that Grandad's dream showed him the future. That's what he was in the end. An empty coat, an outside with nothing left of what he used to be inside. No wonder he looked so confused and ranted and shouted at everyone. I would shout too if I was forgetting who I was and I couldn't do a thing to get me back.

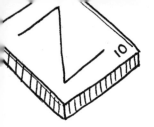

14.

IN THE QUEUE

There are three cars ahead of us now.

Dad lets off the hand brake and we move forward.

Only two cars ahead after that.

"But this car doesn't even need washing!" I tell Dad. "Even Mum said it was really clean."

He looks at me as if I've said something that doesn't make any sense at all.

"I don't ever remember a time your grandad's car was dirty," he says. "It was his pride and joy. Every last Sunday of the month, we took a trip to Moore's Garage. I came here every month from when I was three till I was about your age."

Dad studies a battered old token he has in his hand.

"They haven't changed these, you know. They used the same tokens then – gold, with a shell stamped in the middle. Maybe I even held this one, back then. I thought it was real gold." He sighs and turns the token over and over. "I felt like Charlie Bucket."

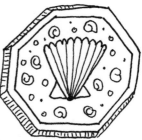

"Who's Charlie Bucket?" I ask.

"You know. The boy with the golden ticket in *Charlie and the Chocolate Factory!*" Dad smiles as if he's telling a joke.

I look at the old token in his hands and I don't see what a token for a car wash has to do with winning a ticket for a trip to a chocolate factory.

But I can see that something is going on with my dad right now.

Dad goes to lift the hand brake again, but then he stops.

"You do it!" he orders me.

I do and it feels weird as the car slides forward. As if I'm in control. I'm laughing.

There is only one car ahead of us now.

It's a people carrier that's crammed full of, well ... people ... loads of kids and a dog that's trying to lick the soap suds off the window from the inside. I can hear screams of excitement through the glass.

"Listen to that. It sounds like they're at the fun fair!" Dad says. "I can't believe I never thought to bring you here when you were little."

I look up at the metal frame of the car wash and try to work out how it all fits together.

The people carrier has to drive between the marked tracks.

A light flashes on red, then amber.

When it's in place there's a loud click and the car gets lowered into a kind of cradle.

Then a green light clicks on and I start counting down.

"Trust me, it's 5 minutes 42 seconds," Dad says. "I counted every second of it, every time we came here. You want to put the token in when it's our go?" He holds it up for me to take.

I'm not all that bothered. I don't feel like Charlie Bucket. How old does Dad think I am? Sometimes he treats me like a baby, Zed. It's like he's forgotten that I'm at secondary school now.

"I remember the first time I came here with your grandad," Dad goes on. "Just about my earliest memory. I thought something magic was going to happen ... 'Put the token in then!' your grandad said, and he let me think that I'd released the hand brake. I wasn't anywhere near strong enough, of course. Hand brakes used to be big heavy levers here in the middle." Dad reaches into the space between our seats.

"There's nothing there," I tell him.

"That's where it used to be. Everything's different these days." Dad sighs.

Lever or not, something is happening to the car right now as it drops into the cradle and shunts forward. I check my phone for the time. It's 16.00 on the dot.

The posts at the side clunk out of place and start to travel towards us on grids of metal.

Fringed propellers – they look like blue tutus – twirl and spin.

Dad laughs and wipes his eyes.

"In the early days I screamed and screamed for your grandad to let me out," he tells me. "I said I wanted to 'get away from the blue monster' – that's what I called it. But he said we couldn't get out, that we were stuck here for the whole 5 minutes. That's how I know, because when the green light came on your grandad said, 'No more crying, son. It's all over now!' But it wasn't ... it takes another 42 seconds to release the car back down so you can drive away."

I don't know what I'm supposed to say to Dad when he's babbling on about nothing. He's never this chatty. So I do what Louis coaches me to do when I can't understand what's expected of me.

'Give yourself a bit of space to try and work out what is going on,' I hear Louis say in my head.

"I got over the fear of course," Dad says. "In fact, I spoke my first words in here. *More! More! More!* Dad used to joke to Mum about how clever I was to read the sign and know the name of Moore's Garage, but really I just wanted to go back through the car wash again. Those were the best times."

Dad looks at me as If he's expecting me to say something. "Clever! Like father, like son," he says.

I think that's supposed to mean we're like each other, or maybe that Grandad was like Dad ... I'm not sure.

79

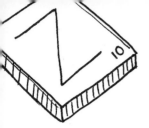

15.

BREAKING THROUGH

One of the overhead metal wipers keeps coming closer and closer to the windscreen in jerks. For a minute it looks like it's going to break the glass.

"I brought Grandad back here not that long ago – to see if it would spark any memories," Dad says.

"Did it?" I ask.

Dad shakes his head. "It was a disaster," he says. "Funny how things turn full circle. I'd left it too long and he cried like a baby the whole time we were in here. I held him in my arms and cried too, because this is the only place where it felt as if it was just him and me. But I couldn't say that at the funeral, could I? Even with memories of your own dad – there are ones that count and ones that won't pass the test in a place like a church ..."

"What test?" I ask Dad. "Why is there a test?"

"Life's full of tests, Hudson," Dad says and then he goes quiet.

I don't know what it is about being all cosy in this car wash together, but I wish he would keep on talking to me about Grandad. Or about anything really, because it feels good to have the sound of Dad's voice in my ear. I don't want him ever to stop talking to me. I don't even care what the words mean. I wish they would just keep washing over me. Why do things have to end?

My dad talking and talking to me ... it's like the engine of a car that everyone thought was dead but someone's managed to fix it and now it's spluttering back to life. That's what Dad always used to tell me – that he was good at fixing things.

The way he's talking reminds me of me when I start following zed-ish trails ...

"The car wash fear didn't last long!" he says again. "By the time I was four I was begging your grandad to bring me."

Dad puts on a little boy voice –

"Let me push the mirrors in."

"Let me put the token in the slot."

"Let me do the hand brake."

Dad turns to me like he wants me to say something ... but I don't know what.

Soap suds fill the surface of every glass screen. It feels like the car's shrunk to the size of a snow globe and someone's just picked us up and is shaking us about. But it's not snow, it's bubbles that stop us seeing out, so that it feels like we're floating on a massive cloud of them.

"I used to think that if there was a Heaven this is what it would be like," Dad says.

I think about the vicar talking about the Kingdom of Heaven at Grandad's funeral. I wonder if Dad's telling me a joke and if I should laugh.

"What? Heaven would be a car wash!"

Dad sighs. "No! I mean it felt like Heaven being here together, just the two of us."

"You and Grandad?" I ask.

"Me and Grandad then. You and me now."

I nod. I think I know why we're here.

Dad laughs again as if he's just remembered something funny. "This bit with all the froth, we used to call it 'head in the clouds'," he says. "When we were all cocooned inside the froth, we used to dream about where in the world we'd like to go on holiday ... places we wanted to see. Your grandad had this grand plan to visit all the wonders of the world."

"And did he?" I ask.

"No," Dad tells me. "He never really left Coventry. He never strayed that far from the factory either. Poor Dad. He didn't get much of a retirement, did he?"

Octopus arms move from the boot to the bonnet and begin to clear the soap suds and the windows as they stretch across the car.

I check the time on my phone. Almost 5 minutes exactly. I hope Dad's right about the extra 42 seconds.

"Think about it," Dad says. "5 minutes 42 seconds x 12 months of the year x 10 years." He looks like he's trying to work out some maths problem, the kind you get at school.

"Why only ten years?" I ask.

"Don't know really." Dad looks at me. "When I was about your age, 12 or 13 or so ..."

"I'm 14, Dad!"

"OK, 14. I was about your age when me and your grandad stopped talking."

I look at Dad and think about what he's saying. I feel sore inside, like the washers have been scrubbing away at my insides. It hurts so bad, but it feels like something's getting clearer too, so I don't want it to stop.

We sit quiet for a while as we watch the jets of clean water spray over the bonnet, ripple like a river over the screen and then clear. Only a few tiny bubbles are left. I am crying but I don't think Dad can see.

The warm air starts to blow hard and the drops of water evaporate on the screen like bubbles bursting. My tears dry up too.

"About this baby," Dad says. "How pregnant is your mum?"

"Very early days, Louis says."

Dad nods.

The dryers are on full now.

Lifting the car

Buffeting us.

Pressure builds on the sides and roof.

Now the wax and polish

Soft sponge pads

Pressed close.

"Once I got over my fear of monsters, you know what I used to wish?" Dad whispers, like this is our secret. "That the 42 seconds would never come ... that me and my dad could just sit in the middle of this car wash all day."

"I wish that too," I whisper back.

Red

Amber

Green

I check my phone and count down from 42 to 1. Dad was right. 5 minutes and 42 seconds is the exact amount of time it took to get through the car wash.

And ...

5 minutes and 42 seconds is the exact amount of time it took for Dad to tell me about his car wash wish. He hasn't talked that much to me in ages.

Now we're out he's gone all quiet again.

Dad stares straight ahead as a bright white light blasts through the windscreen.

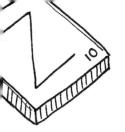

16.

TAKE THE LIGHT AND PASS IT ON

Dad starts the engine, follows the track and goes to drive out of the garage.

He opens his window to push out his side mirror and points for me to do the same.

"What happened to your school badge?" Dad asks, and he points down at my pocket.

"Mum unpicked it, to make it look more like a normal suit. It doesn't, does it?" I ask.

"No!" Dad agrees and squints into the sun. Then he pulls down his sun guard.

"This is how I always remember it!" Dad says and he bashes the steering wheel. "When we drove in, the weather was always dull, and when we came out the sun was always shining."

"*Take the light and pass it on,*" I say.

Dad slams his foot on the brake.

"What did you say?"

"That was the Latin on my school blazer ... the words on the crest that Mum picked off."

I point to the blank shield shape on my pocket. "That's what the school motto means. Take the light and pass it on."

Dad's staring at me, and at the gap on my blazer. Then he seems to change his mind about driving off. He reverses and parks in the waiting bay again.

"What are you doing now?" I ask him. "We're already too late!"

Dad turns to me and gives me this really weird grin. His eyes are all sparkly as if the car wash has shined something up in him too.

"No, I don't think we are, Hudson. We're not too late to get our wish. We're going to be just in time."

I have no idea what he means.

He opens the door and leaves the engine running. Then he runs out, chats a bit to the old man, Mr Moore. Mr Moore throws back his head, laughs and claps Dad on the back as if he's congratulating him for something. It makes me wonder if Dad is actually pleased for Mum and Louis about you, Zed.

Then I realise, Zed, that it's the first time I've thought about you since we drove into this car wash. It's just been me and my dad and it looks like that's how it's going to be again for another whole 5 minutes and 42 seconds.

Dad jumps back in the car, slams the door and drives back around to the car wash.

"Go on, Hudson!" he almost shouts. "You do the honours this time." And he hands me the battered gold token.

I lean over Dad to place it in the slot. He keeps hold of my hand and we both press "START".

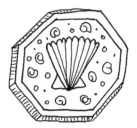

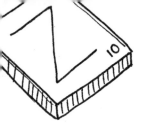

17.

ONE BIG MAP

When I get home I look up the history of the Shell logo. This is how I know the kind of things that other people don't. It says –

In 1891 Marcus Samuel and Company first used the trade mark "Shell" for the kerosene they shipped to the Far East. This London business also sold exotic sea shells. These were so popular on Victorian trinket boxes that soon they formed the basis of the company's trade with the Far East.

In 1897 Samuel formed the Shell Transport and Trading Company. The first logo was a mussel shell, but by 1904 the famous scallop shell emblem gave the brand its visual identity.

I could really get into how these logo, emblem and crest things work. I can see that once you get going everything turns into one big map that shows you how all the roads connect up. You can be travelling along, seeing all these things – like lights and shells – and when you get to the place you've always dreamed of going and look back, it all connects together and makes some sense. This big, joined-up map is the opposite of what happened to Grandad's mind.

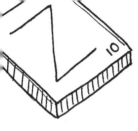

18.

ONE YEAR TO THE DAY

Date: 5th August
Name: Zadie Walters
Gender: Female
Weight: 7 lb 2 oz

Hudson River, New York

15th November
(one year to the day since Grandad's funeral)

Dear Mum, Louis and Zadie

Today Dad gave me a box covered in little shells. He says it's called a trinket box and that it used to be Grandad's. I'm not sure what trinkets are, but inside this box are train tickets and some old photos and a golden token with a shell stamped on it ... a car wash token.

Dad and me threw it into the river.

"To the Hudson, from Hudson, for Grandad." That's what Dad said. Then we both closed our eyes and made a wish. I can't tell you what I wished for, or it might not come true.

Love from Hudson
(the person – not the river!)

P.S. Dad thinks I made an actual joke with that thing I said about my name and the river. I don't think I've ever done that before.

It's a first!

SITA BRAHMACHARI has written lots of brilliant novels about families, love and difference, including ...

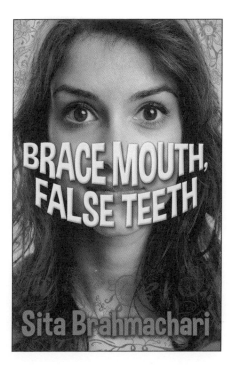

BRACE MOUTH, FALSE TEETH

Sita Brahmachari

What do a former jazz musician, a retired barrister and a one-time Selfridges shop-girl all have in common?

They're the people Zeni is stuck with on her work experience. Zeni wonders how she'll get through her week at Magnolia Gardens Care Home. At least she has Joe to keep her company.

But as the week goes on, Zeni is surprised to find that she makes firm friends with the residents of Magnolia Gardens and before long she is helping them grow old disgracefully!

Our books are tested
for children and young people by
children and young people.

Thanks to everyone who consulted on
a manuscript for their time and effort in
helping us to make our books better
for our readers.